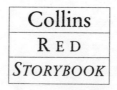

Collins
RED
STORYBOOK

PUMPKIN'S

LEON ROSSELSON

ILLUSTRATED BY VICTOR AMBRUS

Collins

An Imprint of HarperCollinsPublishers

First published in Great Britain by Collins in 2000
Collins is an imprint of HarperCollins*Publishers* Ltd,
77-85 Fulham Palace Road, Hammersmith,
London W6 8JB

The HarperCollins website address is
www.**fire**and**water**.com

1 3 5 7 9 8 6 4 2

Text copyright © Leon Rosselson 2000
Illustrations copyright © Victor Ambrus 2000

ISBN 0 00 675472 4

The author and illustrator assert the moral right to
be identified as author and illustrator of the work.

Printed and bound in Great Britain by
Caledonian international Book Manufacturing Ltd,
Glasgow G64

Contents

PUMPKIN'S DOWNFALL

It was a long time ago and to think of it now is like a weight on my heart. But perhaps by telling it, I shall feel lighter.

Her name was Sara. She was a tall awkward girl with a dreamy smile. And she was slow. Very slow. If you asked her a question, she would gaze at you for ages and then she would look up into the sky and even then sometimes she wouldn't answer but would burst out laughing as if your question was the funniest thing she'd ever heard. You could never tell what she was thinking or if she was thinking at all.

So you see she could be very annoying. This is not to excuse what we did but, at least, you should understand why it happened.

She lived alone with her mother, and even her mother found her exasperating sometimes. She would send Sara to the village shop to buy eggs or strawberry jam and the silly girl would come back with a tin of sardines or a bag of potatoes or else nothing at all. Occasionally, she would disappear for hours until her mother became frantic with worry. Then when she finally came home, still smiling her dreamy smile, she would explain that she'd been having a long conversation with a bird in the wood or a vixen had invited her back to her lair to see her new cubs.

We didn't know whether to believe her about the birds and the animals. She talked about them as if they were her friends, as if they had conversations with her. I suppose she just imagined it. But it was true that she loved animals and birds and that they didn't seem frightened of her. There was a fierce Alsatian dog in the village belonging to the Bell Inn. We used to see it chained to a tree outside the inn and if any of us came too near it, it would growl and snarl and bare its teeth and look as if it was getting ready to spring at us and tear us to pieces. We were terrified of it. But Sara didn't seem to understand that the dog was dangerous. She'd go right up and sit down next to it and pat its head and sing to it in a funny voice. It was weird because instead of biting her, the dog would wag its tail and rub its head against her and lick her face.

So you see, Sara was different. I suppose that was why we teased her and made fun of her. At first, it was just name calling. We started following her around and calling her

silly Sara and stupid Sara, things like that.
Someone – I think it was Caterina – made up a
rhyme which went:

angry. I don't think she even realised she was
being teased most of the time. While we were
following her and calling her names, she'd be
lazing along smiling, as if in a dream, giving
no sign that she knew we were there. When
she did sometimes turn round and see us
making faces at her and mocking her, instead
of being upset and crying, she'd only clap her
hands and laugh.

Of course, that made us even more annoyed.

Pumpkin – that wasn't his real name but
that's what everybody called him – Pumpkin was
the smartest and toughest of us so we looked up
to him as our leader. He said we had to teach
Sara a lesson. So we started playing tricks on her.

When she was walking home from school through the park, Sara had a habit of stopping and standing stock still and staring upwards at a bird in the sky or the top of a tree. We never really knew what she was staring at but she'd often stand there without moving for as long as ten minutes. So Pumpkin got a rope and, while she was standing staring upwards as if she was in a trance, he tied her ankles together. Of course, when she started walking again, she fell over and we all pointed at her and laughed at her and chanted insults. But even that didn't make her angry. She laughed as loudly as any of us and, sprawled on the grass, she sang to herself as she tried to unpick the knots in the rope.

Another time, we tied string between two trees and across the path which we took to go home from school. Then we told Sara we'd race her home and we let her run ahead so that she tripped over the string and went flying. I remember she scraped her knees quite badly that time.

Our favourite trick was to get her to give us her pocket money or her dinner money. It was easy because she believed whatever we told her. Though we tricked her again and again, she never stopped believing the stories we made up, however stupid or unlikely they were. One of us only had to ask her in a sad voice for money to buy flowers for a grandmother's funeral and she would hand over all the money she had on her. And yet nothing that we said to her or did to her ever seemed to shake her good humour.

And it wasn't just us boys who were being so mean to her. The girls were just as bad. After all, wasn't it Caterina who put the dead spider in her milk at lunch time?

Look, you may not believe this, but I never wanted to tease her or make fun of her. I didn't enjoy it. In fact, I felt sorry for her. I thought what we were doing was cruel. But everyone else was doing it so I followed them because I didn't want to be left out. I was one of the youngest and smallest, you see, and if I hadn't joined in, they might have picked on me.

But I was telling you about the spider in her milk. We thought that in her dreamy way, she wouldn't even notice it and would just swallow it down. Then we could all have had a good laugh. But she did notice it. She stared at it for ages, a rather disgusting scrunched-up shape floating blackly in her glass of milk, while we watched her and wondered what she was going to do. She didn't scream. She didn't seem disgusted. She just seemed sad. For once, there was no smile on her face. A tear trickled

When she came back, she told us that Sara had taken the spider into the park and buried it under a rhododendron bush and had sung a mournful little song for it afterwards. I told you she was weird.

Sara didn't come back to school that afternoon. Her mother wrote a note to say that Sara had a bad headache but we knew that wasn't true. When she came back the next day, she wouldn't talk to us. She wouldn't even look at us. It wasn't because we'd been playing tricks on her. She didn't mind that. It was because we'd killed a spider. She loved birds and animals, you see. And insects. When Pumpkin tried to wheedle some money out of her, she just stared at him, or rather stared through him as if he wasn't there, as if he was invisible.

Chapter Two

That was the turning point. That was when everything changed. Some of us had had enough but were too frightened of what Pumpkin would say to do anything about it. It was only when we were gathered in the park after school and Pumpkin was explaining to us gleefully all the things we could do to make Sara's life a misery, that Tim and his sister, Jan, rebelled.

"I've got a catapult I can kill birds with," Pumpkin was boasting. "We can get a dead bird and wrap it up in pretty paper and give it to her as a present."

"No," Tim almost shouted. "We should leave her alone."

Pumpkin was taken aback. "What do you mean?" he asked aggressively.

"Tim's right," Jan said. "She hasn't done anything to us. We should leave her in peace now."

Pumpkin was furious, especially when more children spoke up supporting Tim and Jan. I was surprised and relieved to know that other children felt the same as me. I didn't dare say anything but I moved closer to the rebels to show I was on their side. Pumpkin sneered at us and called us softies and cowards and said we'd be sorry. In the end, most of the children just walked away leaving three boys and two girls to follow Caterina and Pumpkin.

What happened after that was so strange you probably won't believe it. Or you'll think that because it was a long time ago, I'm not remembering it properly. But I do remember it. I remember it as if it was yesterday. If I close

alone in a corner of the playground staring intently at something in the distance. I can see Pumpkin walking up to her, a smirk on his face, and handing her a parcel. We knew then that he'd done what he said he was going to do. He'd killed a bird with his catapult and had wrapped it up in pretty paper.

All the children in the playground stopped playing, stopped what they were doing and turned to watch. I couldn't quite hear what Pumpkin said to her. I think it was something like: "Here's a present for you, Sara." Sara took the parcel and stared at it for a long time. She didn't smile but I thought she had a pleased expression on her face.

"Aren't you going to open it?" Pumpkin asked.

Carefully, Sara took off the pretty wrapping paper. Inside was a cardboard box. She lifted the lid of the box and stared at what was inside. We knew what it was. It was a dead bird. The playground was a pool of silence. Nobody moved. It was as if we'd all been turned to stone.

Pumpkin began to laugh nastily. "What's the matter, Sara? Don't you like your present?" he shouted.

Tears were pouring down Sara's face. Her nose was running. I felt like crying myself. How could Pumpkin be so horrible?

Pumpkin obviously did. He clapped his hands to his ears and ran to the other end of the playground as if he was trying to escape from Sara's scream, as if the scream had cut right through his head and was a burning pain inside it. He crouched down in a corner, his hands still over his ears, and rocked from side to side as if he was in terrible agony.

Sara carried the box with the dead bird in it out of the playground and into the park. All the children followed her. She scraped out a hole in the earth underneath the rhododendron bush and buried the bird there. It was only a small brown bird – a sparrow, probably. Then she sat cross-legged on the grass next to the bird's grave and began to sing a mournful little song. And something strange happened then, too, because I suddenly noticed a cluster of small brown birds perched in the rhododendron bush, not singing, not moving, not fluttering or flying, just perched there like dark silent mourners at a funeral.

I thought that would be the end of it. After that, Pumpkin's gang, even Caterina, deserted him so I thought he would give up playing nasty tricks on Sara. But he didn't. He was furious with everyone and especially with Sara. He said she'd put a spell on him which had given him a terrible pain in his head. I don't see how she could have done that. I think maybe he was making it up. Or else it was just coincidence that he'd got a pain in his head at that moment. Anyway, he said she was going to be sorry for what she'd done.

As long as I've known Pumpkin, he's never looked happy. His face has always had a squeezed, sour expression. But now his face was even more screwed up, his expression even more angry. I was frightened and, at the same time, a bit sorry for him.

A week passed. Then Sara's cat disappeared.

certainly loved that cat. We'd often see her sitting outside her house, the cat on her lap, stroking it and talking to it. And sometimes when she was walking about the village,

the cat would be draped over her shoulder. She came to school once with the cat on her shoulder but the teacher said it wasn't allowed and she had to take it back home. Sara said she'd forgotten the cat was on her shoulder when she walked to school.

When the cat disappeared, Sara became very agitated which wasn't like her. She was usually slow-moving and dreamy. But now she was rushing here and there looking for the cat, calling the cat. And she was asking over and over again: "Have you seen my cat? Have you seen my cat?" It did have a name but I've forgotten it. She just called it Puss. Anyway, nobody had seen her cat. Of course, we all suspected that Pumpkin was behind the cat's disappearance but he wasn't saying anything.

Then on Friday morning, when we were in the playground waiting for school to start, Pumpkin took me aside and told me to give Sara a message. "Tell her if she wants her cat, she'd better meet me by the great oak tree in Gallowstree Wood tomorrow at midday."

I don't know why he chose me as his messenger. Perhaps it was because I was the smallest and he knew I wouldn't refuse.

"Sara," I said, "Pumpkin's got your cat. If you want it back, you'd better go to the great oak tree in Gallowstree Wood at midday tomorrow. Like I said. Do you understand, Sara?"

She didn't say anything. She just kept shaking her head as if she was trying to shake the worry out of it.

"Tomorrow," I said. "That's Saturday. At midday. Twelve o'clock. By the great oak tree in Gallowstree Wood. Don't forget. You'll get your cat back then. OK?"

At last she stopped shaking her head and gave a nod.

"Sorry, Sara," I said. "It's not my fault."

Then I ran to tell Tim and Jan what Pumpkin had said.

"If he's killed her cat," Jan said, "Sara's going to go mad."

By the time the bell rang for school, nearly all the children knew about the meeting in the wood. And, of course, they were all curious to know what was going to happen. So I knew there was going to be a big crowd of kids by the great oak tree the next day.

Chapter Three

I was one of the last to arrive. That Saturday was a dark, gloomy day and my mum said that there was going to be a storm and I shouldn't go out. But I slipped out anyway. When I got there, I saw thirty or forty children standing with their backs to me in a semi-circle round the old oak tree. I couldn't see Sara there. And I didn't see Pumpkin at first. Then when I joined the semi-circle, I saw him. He was standing in front of the tree, one hand in his trouser pocket, looking defiant. What I saw next made my heart jump. Above his head, tied by its hind legs to a branch and hanging upside down, was Sara's cat. I thought at first it was dead. Then it started wriggling and squirming and miaowing piteously so obviously, it wasn't. But it couldn't escape and soon gave up trying. It just hung there helplessly, upside down like a rabbit in a butcher's shop, swaying in the breeze.

"Why did you do it, Pumpkin?" Tim asked.

"'Cause I hate cats," Pumpkin said.

There was an uneasy silence. Someone was going to have to climb up the tree and get the cat down before Sara arrived. But who? Even though we were forty against one, we were all scared of Pumpkin. Long afterwards, I tried to work out what it was about him that frightened us. After all, he wasn't that much bigger and stronger than any of us. What it was, I think, was that he didn't understand about rules. I don't mean rules that grown-ups make to tell you what you should or shouldn't do. I mean the sort of rules you just know

without anyone telling you because they're
inside, inside your head. But Pumpkin didn't
seem to have any rules inside his head. So

While each of us was waiting for someone else to make the first move, Sara ran up. She was out of breath, her nose was red and her hair was in even more of a mess than usual. The semi-circle of children parted to let her through. She saw Pumpkin, stopped, and stood there panting, catching her breath. She hadn't noticed the cat but now it started miaowing again and wriggling around, trying to escape. When Sara saw it she gave a little scream and clapped her hands to her ears as if to block out the plaintive sound of the cat's cries.

Pumpkin bared his teeth in a malicious grin. "What's the matter, Sara?" he said. "It's only a mangy old cat."

It was at that moment I remember hearing a rumble of thunder, and a few drops of rain spat down.

Sara ran towards the cat and jumped up to reach it but it was much too high. The best way to get it down was to climb up the tree and along the branch which was what Pumpkin must have done. Meanwhile the cat was becoming more and more frantic, wriggling and squirming and making a whining noise like a baby. What we should

stood there watching, paralysed. It was as if this was between Sara and Pumpkin and it wasn't for us to interfere.

There was another louder rumble of thunder. The sky grew darker.

Sara, realizing she couldn't reach the cat, ran to the tree and tried to climb it but she wasn't agile enough.

"You'll never climb that tree," Pumpkin taunted. "You're too clumsy."

Then he took his hand out of his trouser pocket and we could see that he was holding his catapult. "I hate cats," he snarled. "I hate everything." And he bent down to pick up a stone.

Sara turned from the tree and pointed a finger at him. "You—" she began. "You—" But her tongue seemed to stick and she couldn't get any more words out.

"Go on, spit it out," Pumpkin sneered. He put the stone in the catapult and stepped back a bit to take aim at the cat.

"You – be—" stuttered Sara.

"You – be—" mocked Pumpkin.

He stepped backwards and pulled the elastic on the catapult. A leafy branch was in the way so he moved to the left and further back to get a clearer view of the cat. Then he took aim.

That moment seemed to last for ages. Picture the scene if you can. Sara pointing her finger at Pumpkin, trying to say something that would stop him but unable to tumble the words out of her mouth. Pumpkin with the catapult drawn back ready to fire the stone at the cat. The cat still wriggling and squirming and making a melancholy yowling noise. And the semi-circle of children waiting and

watching, unable to do anything. I felt sick.
My knees were trembling.

The next moment, something happened
which seemed so strange we couldn't take it in.
At last, Sara managed to blurt the words out.

"You – be – gone!" she shouted.

There was a dazzling flash of lightning and
Pumpkin was – gone. A stone hit the trunk of
the tree and rattled to the ground. There was
an even louder roll of thunder.

We stared amazed at where Pumpkin had
been. He seemed to have disappeared
completely, vanished into thin air. Had he been

struck by lightning? Had Sara made him invisible by magic? Or had he run away so fast we hadn't seen him go? We didn't know what

branch from which the cat was hanging. He crawled along the branch, untied the cat and dropped it into Sara's waiting arms.

She clasped it to her and kissed it and stroked it and made soothing noises to it. The smile returned to her face. Then she gave us all a little bow and said, "Thank you. Thank you."

I felt ashamed. Why was she thanking us? We hadn't done anything. We hadn't tried to rescue the cat until Pumpkin had gone. We hadn't tried to stop Pumpkin firing a stone at the cat. We'd done nothing to help her.

"What happened?" Jan asked. "Where's Pumpkin?"

"Gone," Sara said and laughed. Then she thanked us again and set off for home, carrying the cat in her arms and singing to it in her funny voice.

My mother had been right. There was a storm. The rain came down in buckets. By the time I reached home, I was soaking, and my mum gave me a sharp telling off.

Chapter Four

We all wondered what had happened to Pumpkin. I suppose you're wondering as well. Did Sara have some magic power that made him disappear? Many of the children thought that. They looked at Sara differently from then on as someone to be respected. Tim and Jan became very friendly with her. They sort of adopted her. They were always going around together. They said she was slow, yes, but she wasn't at all as silly as she seemed. She knew the names of every bird and flower and where the little fox cubs played and which were the mushrooms you could eat and where the bees made their honey and how to talk to horses. And now that she had friends, she became less awkward and more talkative.

As for Pumpkin, he hadn't disappeared for ever. He wasn't seen that weekend but he turned up at school on Monday morning. He seemed strangely subdued. His face and arms were covered in scratches and he was limping. He refused to talk about what had happened. And our attitude towards him changed. He seemed different. Whether it was magic or not, in our eyes, he'd been defeated by Sara so we lost our fear of him. And because he couldn't bully us any more, he changed, too. If he hadn't, he'd always have been an outcast.

So was it magic when the lightning flashed and Pumpkin disappeared? That depends. I

don't think it was Sara saying "You be gone" that did it. I went back to Gallowstree Wood a few days later and found the place where I thought Pumpkin had been standing when he disappeared. Behind him was a downwards slope covered in ferns and at the bottom of the slope was a bramble patch. I caught sight of something hanging from a bramble bush that looked very much like Pumpkin's catapult. When I stepped into the ferns I put my foot down a large hole, a fox's hole, maybe, or a rabbit's. Then I realised what must have happened. The flash of lightning and Sara shouting "You be gone" must have startled Pumpkin just as he was about to fire off the stone. He must have stepped backwards, put his foot in the hole, lost his balance and tumbled down into the brambles. Maybe he hit his head, too, which knocked him out and that's why he didn't climb back up again straight away.

So it wasn't magic. But then again, when I think of what might have happened, if the lightning hadn't flashed just at the right time, if Sara hadn't shouted "You be gone," if Pumpkin hadn't put his foot in the hole and tumbled backwards— . The cat would have been killed. Sara would have gone mad.

Pumpkin would have stayed a bully. But that one moment changed everything for ever. So maybe, in a way, it was magic.

THE MONKEY

Chapter One

We stared at him. We didn't get many children coming to the school from outside the village so we were curious. He had blonde curly hair and looked too small and thin and young to be in our class. The thing I remember most is that his face was blank. Like a mask.

Mrs Grace stood behind him at the front of the class with her hands on his shoulders. "This is Mark," she said. "He's going to be joining us now so please make him welcome."

A whispery sound rustled round the class. To tell the truth, we resented rather than welcomed new arrivals.

"Mark's new to the village," Mrs Grace went on. "He doesn't have any friends yet so I hope you're all going to make him feel at home."

The whisper became a questioning murmur. Who were his parents? Where were they living? Why had he come to the village? Where had he come from?

I said nothing. I couldn't take my eyes off his face. There was no expression on it. He didn't smile or frown or look embarrassed. He didn't seem to be there at all. I thought he was weird. So I wasn't best pleased when Mrs Grace said he would sit next to me because I was going to be the one to look after him and show him around the school.

Tim moved to another seat so that Mark could sit beside me. He didn't look at me. He sat down, put his bag on the desk and opened it. Then he took out – what do you think? No, not an exercise book or a pen or anything like that. He took out a puppet. That's right, a puppet. A glove puppet with a monkey face. I

Mark didn't seem to hear me. He put his right hand in the glove puppet and suddenly it came alive. It waved its arms. It opened its mouth. Then it spoke. "It's all right," it said in a funny, high-pitched voice. "I can look after myself."

Of course, I know puppets can't speak. But Mark had worked the puppet so skilfully, he'd made it seem so lifelike, that for a moment I really believed it was the puppet speaking. I hadn't even seen Mark's lips move.

There was a hushed silence. Everyone was staring at Mark and the monkey puppet and waiting to see what Mrs Grace would do. I looked at her questioningly.

Mrs Grace forced a smile. "Don't worry," she said to me in a low voice. "I'll explain later." Then clapping her hands, she turned to the class and said briskly, "Come along now, it's time we settled down and did some work."

I couldn't believe it. Mrs Grace was usually strict. If anyone brought a toy or a sweet or a comic into the class, she'd confiscate it. Now here was this new boy playing with a puppet and she was letting him get away with it.

Why? What was so special about him? I was furious with Mrs Grace and with the new boy.

I can't remember much about the rest of the speak. Twice, though, when Mrs Grace asked the class a question, he called out the answer. Or rather the monkey puppet did in its funny voice. You weren't supposed to do that. Call out, I mean. You were supposed to put your hand up if you knew the answer. But Mrs Grace didn't rebuke him. She just smiled at him, a bit nervously, I thought. I felt confused and troubled and, to tell the truth, a little frightened of this strange boy.

When break time came, Mrs Grace asked me to stay behind. Mark went out into the playground with the other children. The glove puppet, I noticed, was on his right hand.

"I hope he'll be all right," Mrs Grace

murmured. Then she sat me down in front of her and looked at me with a serious expression on her face. "You're a good boy, Daniel, a sensible boy," she said. "That's why I asked you to look after Mark."

"He's weird," I said.

"Yes," she said. "He is a little strange. But he's not silly. In fact, he's very bright."

"What's the matter with him then?" I asked. "Why has he got that monkey puppet?"

Mrs Grace sighed. "It's not easy to explain," she said. "But I'll tell you what I know about him so you'll understand better. I'm relying on you to be a friend to him, you see. He'll need you to help him and make sure he doesn't get bullied. Will you do that?"

I don't want to sound conceited but I was beginning to feel quite important. After all, out of the whole school, I was the one who'd been chosen to look after this boy.

"I'll try, Mrs Grace," I said.

Mrs Grace smiled. "I'm sure you will," she said. Then she told me that Mark's mother had died a little while ago and since then Mark had become more and more silent. One day, he stopped speaking. No-one could get him to say

Chapter Two

I understood now why Mrs Grace couldn't confiscate the puppet. But I was disappointed. I'd expected something more terrible than that. Other children in the village had fathers or mothers who'd died or who'd gone away. Poor Elizabeth's parents had both died and she'd had to go and live with her grandparents. But she hadn't stopped speaking.

"After his mother died, he lived with his father and his aunt, his father's sister," Mrs

Grace went on. "His father wanted to make a new start. That's why they moved here. They've bought Morton Hall."

there for as long as I can remember had died about a year ago. Since then it had been a ghost house, surrounded by grey stone walls and locked gates. I started to feel sorry for Mark having to live in a place like that.

"His father must be really rich," I said.

"Perhaps," Mrs Grace said. "I met him and the boy's aunt when they brought him into school. And I'm afraid I didn't warm to either of them. But there, I shouldn't be saying things like that. I really know nothing about them."

In my head, I was already concocting a fantastic tale of Mark's wicked father and aunt plotting to take over the world when Mrs Grace's voice brought me back to reality.

"What do you think, Daniel?" she asked.

"He's a good ventriloquist, Mark is," I said. "With that monkey puppet."

Mrs Grace laughed. "Yes, he is," she said. "Apparently, the puppet was a present from his mother but he only started playing with it after she died. But what I was really asking was whether you thought you could be a friend to this strange boy."

I shrugged. "I suppose so," I said.

"I hope so," Mrs Grace said. "Now you'd better go and see how he's getting along with the other children."

I found Mark in a corner of the playground, staring at nothingness. He had that look of not being there at all. The puppet was not on his hand.

"Where's your puppet, Mark?" I asked.

I thought maybe, just maybe, he might decide to speak again. He looked at me but said nothing. His face was pale and he had a frightened look as if I'd just caught him doing something naughty.

I looked around the playground. In another corner, a bunch of children were gathered. I ran over to them. Pumpkin was at the centre

such a bully any more because after the business with Sara's cat we'd stopped being frightened of him. But still, he was bigger and stronger than me so my heart was thumping.

"That's Mark's puppet," I said. "He needs it."

Pumpkin looked at me with that sneer on his face. "What's it got to do with you?" he said.

"I'm supposed to look after him," I said. "He needs the puppet."

"Why's he allowed to bring a puppet to school and we're not?" Pumpkin said.

"He can't speak," I said. "He can't speak except through the puppet."

"What are you talking about?" Pumpkin said.

"It's true," I said. "Mrs Grace told me. He's got special permission to have that puppet. He won't be able to speak if he doesn't have it. He speaks through the puppet."

Pumpkin stared at me as if trying to decide whether I was making it up or not.

"Ask Mrs Grace," I said.

"He's a loony then, isn't he?" Pumpkin said.

I didn't feel like explaining or arguing any

more. "Give me the puppet, please, Pumpkin," I said.

My heart was thumping so loudly I thought

"Better give him it," Tim said.

Pumpkin looked round at the faces of the children and realised that no-one was supporting him.

"I don't want his stupid puppet anyway," he said. Then he threw the puppet on the floor and walked away.

I picked it up, brushed the dust off it and ran back to Mark. "Here's your puppet, Mark," I said.

His face came alive and relaxed into a half-smile. He put the puppet on his hand and said in a voice like Mr Punch, "That's the way to do it."

A shiver ran down my spine. What was I

going to do with this weird boy? How was I going to talk to him, to help him? How could I be friends with a boy who never spoke to me in his own voice? What was the matter with him? Why couldn't he speak normally like the other children? He wasn't dumb. If he could speak in the voice of a puppet, he could speak in his own voice. But he wouldn't. He was just being stubborn. He was just being difficult. Perhaps he just wanted to be different. Why did I have to be the one to look after him?

I went to Mrs Grace to ask her to choose someone else.

"Try for a little longer," she said. "Don't let me down."

"I'll never get used to it," I said. "I'll never get used to that stupid monkey puppet."

"You will," she said.

Chapter Three

And she was right. I suppose you can get used to anything in time. It wasn't long before not only me but all the children in the class, even Pumpkin, were talking to the puppet as if it was alive. Mark was such a good ventriloquist that we almost forgot he was there. It was the monkey puppet that was doing the talking. It had a personality of its own. It was lively, cheeky, funny. It became the class joker, calling out funny things in lessons to make us laugh.

When Mrs Grace said we were going to learn something about water, the monkey puppet called out, "It's wet," and everyone laughed. And when Mrs Grace brought a pumpkin into the room and asked if we knew what it was, the puppet squeaked out, "It's an elephant," and for some reason we all found that very funny. Even Mrs Grace smiled. She couldn't really do anything else. She couldn't confiscate the puppet and I suppose she didn't want to tell Mark off.

So, to my surprise, Mark didn't get made fun of or mocked, as usually happened to any child who was a bit different. I realise now why it was that Mark escaped. It was because in a way he wasn't there at all. Or rather, he was hidden, hidden behind the puppet so nobody could get at him. Maybe that was part of the reason he did it. But only part of the reason.

The puppet would never say anything about Mark. I used to walk home with him sometimes and I'd tell him about my family and how I didn't have a father and how my mother was always worrying about me and things like that. Then I'd ask him about his mother and

monkey puppet would squeak out something silly. I often invited him to my house but he wouldn't come. And he never invited me to his house.

That's how it went and that's how it would have gone on, I suppose, if something hadn't happened to change that. And although what happened seemed terrible at the time, I'm glad now that it did happen because I wouldn't otherwise have discovered the truth about Mark and his monkey puppet. And we would never have become friends – real friends, I mean.

One Monday, a cold wintry day as I remember, Mark didn't come to school. He didn't come the next day either or the next day. We thought he was probably ill. We missed him. Or rather, we missed his cheeky, funny monkey puppet. At the end of the week, Mrs Grace asked me to call in at Morton Hall to see what was the matter. I didn't want to go. I know it's silly to be afraid of a house but there was something about that grey gloomy place that made me shiver. You couldn't imagine children living there, shouting and laughing.

On Saturday morning, I told my mother where I was going – so that if anything happened to me she'd know who to blame – and I set off for Morton Hall.

"Don't be long," she called to me as I was leaving. "And put on your winter coat. It's cold."

"No it's not," I shouted back as I slipped out the door.

But it was. It was freezing, even though a weak watery sun hung low in the sky. I ran shivering all the way up the hill to Morton

Hall and stood in front of the iron gates. Then, summoning up all my courage, I pushed open the gate and scrunched my way up the

reached up to the heavy black knocker and hammered twice on the door. The noise echoed through my head as I stood there shivering.

Footsteps approached on the other side of the door and I prepared myself to run off if I had to. But there was nothing frightening about the woman who opened the door. She was about the same age as my mum, only she was taller and thinner, and her face was hard as if she never smiled. She was, I supposed, Mark's aunt. She looked down at me without speaking.

"Sorry," I said. Why did I feel I had to apologise? Then the words came tumbling out. "I'm a friend of Mark's and Mrs Grace said I should come and see if he was all right."

The woman frowned. "And who are you?" she demanded.

"I'm Daniel," I said. "I'm Mark's friend at school. Mrs Grace sent me—"

"Yes, I heard you the first time," she interrupted. "Mark has been unwell. You can tell your teacher he'll be back at school as soon as he's well enough."

"When will that be?" I asked.

"As soon as he's well enough," she

repeated firmly, preparing to shut the door.

"Can I see him?" I said.

"Certainly not."

me. "I told you to put your winter coat on."

"Sorry," I said, and went to give her a hug. She was soft and round and warm and I was glad she was my mum.

When I went back to school the next Monday, Mrs Grace said that Mark's father had written a letter to explain that his son had a touch of pneumonia and wouldn't be able to return to school until he was fully recovered. I didn't believe it, I don't know why. Maybe it was the gloomy house or the way Mark's hard-faced aunt had refused to allow me to see him or what Mrs Grace had said about not warming to Mark's father and aunt but I felt something was wrong. Dark thoughts cobwebbed my mind. I began to imagine terrible things – I'm ashamed to admit what they were – especially when I was alone or drifting off to sleep. Of course, I didn't tell anyone about them. They'd have called me stupid or mad. Terrible things didn't happen in our village. But I couldn't help it. I couldn't brush the dark imaginings away from my mind.

By the end of that week, Mark still hadn't returned to school. On the Friday, as I was going home, I thought I might make a detour, wander up the hill to Morton Hall, just to take a look. What was I expecting to see? I don't know. I didn't have a plan in mind. I certainly wasn't going to knock at the door again and ask to see Mark. It was only that— What? I can't explain why I went. I just did. Things happen like that sometimes without you even wanting them to happen.

So, in the gathering gloom of a cold winter evening, huddled into my heavy winter coat, I walked slowly up the hill to Morton Hall. As I

approached the house, I saw that the curtains were drawn and there was a light in one of the downstairs windows. The house has got one eye open, I thought to myself. A car was parked in the driveway. I stood outside the gates wondering what to do, wondering what secrets that dark doomy house was hiding, wondering if I dared creep up to the house to see if I could see anything through the windows. As I stood there wondering and staring, the light in the window went out, the door of the house opened and I heard the crunch of footsteps on the driveway. I moved away from the gate and flattened myself against the stone wall. There was the sound of the bolt being drawn back and the gates creaking open. The footsteps crunched back to the house. Without even thinking, I darted inside the gates and onto the grass.

Chapter Four

This is what I saw as I peered out from behind an overgrown rosebush: a big tall man and a tall thin woman silhouetted against the light from the hall. No sign of Mark. Then the hall light went out. I heard the car engine being switched on and saw the car headlights shoot out its beams into the gloom. The car drove out of the gate and stopped. I saw a figure get out of the car, a giant of a man he seemed to me. Mark's father. He was pulling the gates shut and I started to panic. Supposing he locked the gates. How would I escape from the garden? The walls were too high to climb. Could I climb over the gate? Then the man stopped pulling at the gate, said something to the woman inside the car and walked heavily back to the house.

My brain was racing. He's forgotten something in the house, I remember thinking. He's going to go out with Mark's aunt. They're going to leave Mark all by himself. How could they do that? Where was Mark anyway? A light went on in the hallway. I tiptoed closer to the house, then closer still. The front door was ajar. A light went on in an upstairs room. I felt excited, daring, light-headed. I wasn't at all afraid. I felt as if I was in a film and I was the hero. I was the one chosen to rescue Mark from... from what? I didn't know. I only knew

I had to rescue him. Without thinking, I darted into the house, saw that a door to the left was open and slipped inside the room. I crouched

later, I heard the car being driven away. Then silence.

Gradually I became aware of sounds filling the silence. The sound of my own breathing. The beating of my heart. The crackling of a fire in the grate. I stood up. The fire shed a flickery light into the room. I went over to the window and peeped through the curtains. There was no car, no sign of anyone anywhere. Where was Mark? I had to find him.

My eye caught sight of something familiar, half in, half out of the fire. I went over to get a closer look. Surely, it couldn't be— I used a poker to pull it away from the fire. Most of it was burnt but the head was untouched, just a

bit blackened. It was Mark's monkey puppet –
or what was left of it. Suddenly I felt fear in
the pit of my stomach. Who could have
thrown his puppet into the fire? Why would
anyone do that? How would Mark speak
without it? I was sure now Mark was in
danger.

I rushed over to switch on the light in the
room. Then I rushed into the hallway and
switched on the light there. Then into the
kitchen and all the rooms on the ground floor.
The lights blazed out. I didn't care if anyone

outside saw them. I just wanted to drive away the darkness.

As I raced from room to room, I called out,

rattled the door. "Mark! Are you in there?" I called. No sound came from inside the room. Surely he would have made a noise if he was there, even if he didn't speak. He wasn't in his bedroom either. I knew it was his bedroom although there were no posters on the walls, as there were in my bedroom, and no toys either. Just some books, a bed and on the table next to the bed a photograph of a younger Mark with his mother. I picked it up and inspected it. She looked nice, I thought. There was no photograph of his father.

I almost tripped and fell as I raced down the stairs. Mark had to be somewhere in the house. But where? Then, as I stood in the hallway, I heard it. A banging sound. It seemed to be coming from the kitchen. There was a door in there that I'd been in too much of a rush to notice before. Where did it lead to? Someone was banging on the door. I tried to open it but, of course, it was locked. Where was the key?

"Mark!" I called. The banging became more urgent. "I can't open the door. Where's the key?"

The banging stopped. But there was no voice to tell me where the key was. I looked everywhere in the kitchen, in all the cupboards, in all the drawers. I was becoming frantic. What if Mark's father and aunt came back? What was I going to say? They might think that I was a burglar.

Then I saw it. It was hanging on a hook next to the door. How stupid of me not to have seen it before. The key fitted. I unlocked the door and opened it. Steps led down into a cellar. Mark sat hunched on the top step, his head buried in his knees. He was shivering.

"Mark!" I called. "What's the matter? Why have they put you here?"

He stood up and turned towards me. He had that frightened look on his face. He seemed smaller and paler and thinner than ever.

"I'm your friend, Mark. You've got to tell me. You've got to talk."

But Mark said nothing. He just stared at me as if he didn't understand what was happening.

Suddenly I remembered. The monkey

puppet. Or what was left of it. I ran to the room where the fire was and picked up the monkey face and the shreds of blackened cloth. My heart sank. It wasn't going to work. It wasn't going to help him speak. There was no monkey puppet now. The monkey puppet was dead.

Mark had followed me into the room. When he saw the remains of the puppet, his eyes lit up and he took it from me. Was he going to try and make it speak? No. He seemed to be searching for something inside the head. His fingers poked as far as they would go, all around the inside of the monkey head. Then, with a half-smile on his face, he drew out something that he'd found there.

"What is it, Mark?"

He held out his hand to show me. It was a ring, a gold ring with red and white stones. I held it up to the light and saw the stones gleam and sparkle magically.

"It's beautiful," I said. "Whose ring is it?"

But still Mark wouldn't speak. He took the

ring from me and went upstairs. I didn't know
what to do. I didn't know what was happening.
When he came down again, he was wearing

It was stupid. I knew he wasn't going to answer me but still I had to keep asking him questions.

He took hold of my hand and pulled me towards the front door. I opened it and we stepped out into the garden. Then I felt his hand tighten on mine. My heart jumped. The car, headlights on, was drawing up outside the gates. It stopped. Mark's father got out. He seemed bigger and more terrifying than ever. He was pushing open the gates. We were mesmerised. We couldn't move. Now there was no time to hide. He'd seen us. He was walking towards us. We were trapped. Mark pulled his hand away, took something from his pocket and handed it to me. I stared at it. It was the ring.

"What, Mark? What am I supposed to do with it?"

The figure of Mark's father advanced towards us.

And then it happened. Something changed. That's the way it happens sometimes.

Suddenly. Do you know what I mean? Something changes, in a minute, in a second. One minute it's pouring with rain and the next

Daniel."

It was a quiet musical voice, not at all like the voice of the monkey puppet.

"Run, Daniel!" it said again.

Mark's father was looming over us, staring down at us.

"Run, Daniel!"

I ran, evading the man's outstretched arm.

Chapter Five

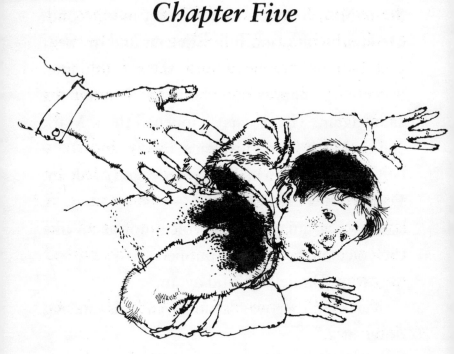

I could have outrun him, I think. I'm a good
runner and he was a heavily-built man. So I
think I could have outrun him. And then
again, everything might have been different.
But I didn't get the chance. As I sprinted
towards the gate, clutching the ring tightly, I
tripped and fell flat on my face. I think I was
distracted because I saw the tall thin figure of

Mark's aunt climbing out of the car. Whatever the reason, I tripped and fell and scraped my hand, which was still holding on to the ring,

the scruff of my neck and turned round. A large, strong hand forced open my fingers and took the ring from me. Then the hand pushed me away.

"Daniel!" a voice called from the darkness. "This way."

I ran towards the voice. Mark took my hand and pulled me towards the gate. We ran out of the gate, past the car, past Mark's aunt.

"Mark!" we heard her call. "Where are you going?"

We ran round and along the wall of the house and then Mark stopped and crouched down, wheezing heavily, trying to catch his breath.

"Sorry," I panted. "The ring. I tripped. He's got the ring."

Mark stood up and looked at me sadly.

"Sorry," I said.

"It's not your fault," he said.

We heard the car being driven through the gates to the house. Then heavy footsteps on the driveway and into the street. In the deep silence of the night, every sound seemed to be magnified.

"Mark!" It was the voice of Mark's father, calling from the street.

We flattened ourselves against the wall and looked at each other.

"Mark!" he called again. "Where are you? Come in at once."

Mark shook his head and put his finger to his lips.

"Come in, Mark, we're not going to punish you."

We stood stock still, two frozen shapes against the grey stone wall, hoping he couldn't see or hear us.

"If you don't come in now, Mark, we're going to lock the gates and you'll have to stay out here all night."

The rustle of the wind was the only answer and a silence that seemed to last for ever. Then we heard the sound of the gates being pushed shut and heavy footsteps walking back to the house.

I looked at Mark questioningly.

"If I go back," he said, "they'll lock me in the cellar again."

"But he's your father— " I began.

"He's not my father," Mark said. "He's not my father."

Chapter Six

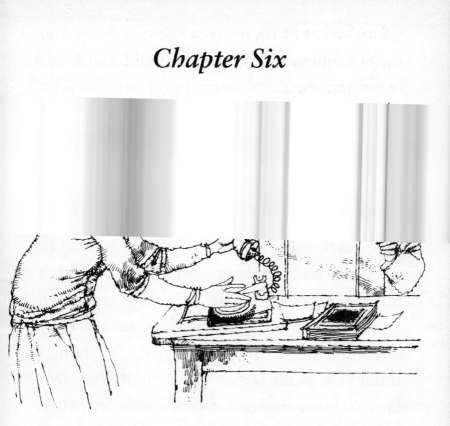

Of course, Mark came home with me. And, of course, my mum was frantic with worry because I was late coming home from school. She'd been to the school to look for me and was just about to phone for the police. I would probably have been told off except that she was so relieved that I was safe. And then there was Mark and there were the questions and the explanations. I tried to tell her as much as I could but she didn't seem to understand who Mark was and why he was there. But she said he was welcome to stay the night and made a bed up for him in my room and gave us supper and sent us off to bed.

It was as we were lying in bed that night that Mark told me for the first time some of the things that had happened to him. He didn't tell me everything. He wouldn't say much about his mother dying. And he wouldn't say anything about his real father. The man I thought was his father was actually his step-father. He'd married Mark's mother when Mark was about six. Mark said he'd never liked him.

"I told her I didn't like him and I didn't want her to marry him. She laughed and kissed me and said I'd grow to like him in time. But I never did. When she died, he asked his horrible sister to help look after me."

"Is that when you started talking through

the monkey puppet?" I asked.

"I didn't want to talk to them," he said. "I missed my mum. They were horrible to me.

"What if I did? It was their fault. I didn't want to live with them. They said I was spoilt. They said children should be seen and not heard. So I stopped talking to them."

"Why didn't you talk to us?" I asked.

Mark seemed to think for a bit about this. Then he said, "I was afraid."

"What of?"

"In case I got found out."

"What do you mean?"

"In case you found out who I was."

"I don't understand."

"The monkey puppet was funny," Mark said. "I'm not funny. I'm not anything."

I think I understand now what he meant by that. It's like I said before, he was sort of hiding behind the puppet. But at the time I didn't really know what he was talking about.

"What about the ring?" I said. "Whose ring is it?"

"It belonged to my mum," Mark said. "She inherited it from her mum with some other jewellery and some money and the house."

"What house?"

"Morton Hall," Mark said.

"Morton Hall?" I was amazed.

"They never lived in it. They just owned it.

When she died, he got everything, the house, the money, me, everything. I wanted the ring because it was beautiful. And it reminded me.

"Did they punish you?"

"I didn't care," said Mark, "I wasn't speaking to them. My puppet was speaking for me and he wouldn't tell them where the ring was. They didn't seem to care very much at the beginning. Then he gave up his job and we moved here and I think they spent a lot of money on the house and the furniture, and he said I had to give him the ring. He said it wasn't any use to anyone and he needed it. He said I'd be locked in the cellar till I told them where it was. My puppet told them that he didn't know anything about the ring but that just made them more angry. In the end, the puppet said it was in my desk at school.

I just wanted them to leave me alone. I didn't think they'd go to the school and see if it was there."

"They never guessed that the puppet had the ring all the time," I said admiringly.

"They're stupid, that's why," Mark said.

"What will they do with the ring now?" I asked.

"Sell it," he said. "They want the money. That's all they want. Money."

"Is it very valuable then?"

"I suppose so," Mark said.

"So," I said, "if you had the ring, you'd be rich."

"I wouldn't sell it," Mark almost shouted. "I'd never sell it."

And then he burst into tears. He just sobbed and sobbed and wouldn't stop. I'd never heard anyone cry so much. I couldn't think of anything to say to him. There was nothing I could say to him. I remember thinking, just before I drifted off to sleep, I remember thinking how lucky I was and how unlucky

Mark had been.

Mark stayed. Where else could he go? He wouldn't go back to his stepfather and his

brother I never had.

Are you wondering if he ever stopped speaking again? No, he didn't. And he never played with a puppet again either, which was a shame because he was such a good ventriloquist. But he said he didn't need puppets any more because he was going to speak in his own voice. The funny thing is that he was completely different from his monkey puppet. The puppet was cheeky and funny. Mark was always polite and very serious. Isn't that strange?

It's strange, too, how things turned out. When I think back, I often ask myself what would have happened if I hadn't gone to Morton Hall that day after school. What would have happened if— ? What if— ? Have you ever asked yourself that question? If you have, you'll know that there'll never be an answer.

THE WITCH'S TEARS
by Jenny Nimmo

travels. But the blizzard continues and the night
is long... and there may be tears before morning.

*Another Collins Red Storybook
to add to your collection!*

Collins

An Imprint of HarperCollins*Publishers*
www.fireandwater.com

Order Form

To order direct from the publishers, just make a list of the titles you want and fill in the form below:

Name ....

Address ....

....

....

Send to: Dept 6, HarperCollins Publishers Ltd, Westerhill Road, Bishopbriggs, Glasgow G64 2QT.

Please enclose a cheque or postal order to the value of the cover price, plus:

UK & BFPO: Add £1.00 for the first book, and 25p per copy for each additional book ordered.

Overseas and Eire: Add £2.95 service charge. Books will be sent by surface mail but quotes for airmail despatch will be given on request.

A 24-hour telephone ordering service is available to holders of Visa, MasterCard, Amex or Switch cards on 0141- 772 2281.

Collins
An *Imprint of* HarperCollins*Publishers*